SNOW

STEVE SANFIELD

ILLUSTRATED BY

JEANETTE WINTER

PHILOMEL BOOKS • NEW YORK

Text copyright © 1995 by Steve Sanfield

Illustrations copyright © 1995 by Jeanette Winter

All rights reserved. This book, or parts thereof, may not be reproduced

in any form without permission in writing from the publisher.

Philomel Books, a division of The Putnam & Grosset Group,

200 Madison Avenue, New York, NY 10016.

Philomel Books, Reg. U.S. Pat. & Tm. Off.

Published simultaneously in Canada.

Printed in Hong Kong by South China Printing Co. (1988) Ltd.

Book design by Gunta Alexander. The text is set in Icone.

Library of Congress Cataloging-in-Publication Data

Sanfield, Steve. Snow / Steve Sanfield;

illustrated by Jeanette Winter. p. cm.

Summary: Everything is different the morning after a deep new snowfall.

[1. Snow — Fiction.] I. Winter, Jeanette, ill. II. Title. PZ7.S2237Sn

1995 [E]— dc20 94-8754 CIP AC ISBN 0-399-22751-2

1 3 5 7 9 10 8 6 4 2

First Impression

Somewhere in the distance
of this chilly night
an owl calls.

Waking this morning
to find the world
covered in white.

All the world
a single color
— even the sky.

The dry grasses
seen afresh
after a night of snow.

Limbs cracking.
Branches snapping.
Snow doing its work.

Sailing ships and skyscrapers
shaped
by the shifting snow.

Not even barking dogs
penetrate this wall of snow
—the hush of it.

Bent to the ground
that plum tree I planted
on my birthday.

Under deep ice
the sound
of rushing water.

A black cat
makes the snow
whiter.

So much snow
who can remember
when it began?

Sliding from one branch
to another
and still another.

On moonlit snow
even my shadow
is cold.

Never brighter
never farther away
—the winter stars.

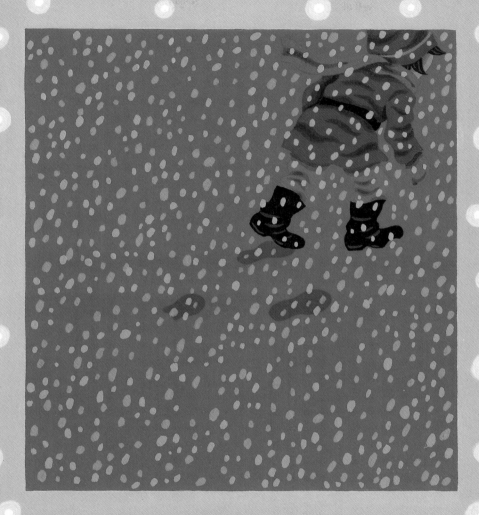

Even before returning
my tracks
are covered.

Light in a blizzard
even friendlier
because it's my house.

Midnight.
Snow still falling.
No one going anywhere.

All night long
thousands of snowflakes
gathering on the roof.

Tracks in the snow:
what happened
while I slept.

After the storm
walking in the woods
listening to the silence.

Suddenly the sparkling sun
but still cold
—so very cold.

The snow falls
only for itself
this last night of the year.

The power of snow
to make all things
new.